Molly's Story

by Linda Wyon
illustrations by Angela Goodman

Foreword

Child contact centres are a wonderful idea. They're safe, supportive places where children can enjoy contact with parents and other family members they've been separated from.

Molly's brilliant story gives us a real flavour of what goes on in a child contact centre and how important it is to stay in touch.

When you've read the book, find out where your nearest centre is and support it!

[signature]

Dr Phil Hammond
GP, Writer and Broadcaster

Molly was worried.
Mummy had stopped smiling.

Before Tom was born they were all
so excited at the thought of a new baby.

Now things were different.

Mum had warned her that babies cry
when they are hungry but even when
Tom yelled she didn't seem to hear him.

Molly often had to go and find Daddy.

One day when they got home from school, Dad said
'Sorry Moll, Mum's gone away for a bit.'

Molly cried and asked 'Where?'

She simply didn't understand.

Dad told her not to worry, that Mum would probably be back soon.

But Mum didn't come back and Molly did worry.

Although she loved Dad to bits, she still loved Mummy
and remembered all the things they used to do together.

Was it her fault that Mum had left?

She didn't like to talk about it with Dad, because he always seemed busy.....
but she hadn't seen Mum for ages and wondered if she would ever see her again!

When Tommy was in bed, Daddy would read to her. Of course Molly could read to herself now but she still loved to snuggle up at bedtime and listen, as the stories came alive.

She often thought of Mummy and how she had always made it a very special time...

Tonight was different.

Dad said that instead of a story he wanted to talk. It sounded serious and Molly must have looked **very** worried because Dad said 'Hey, don't pull that face, this could be good!'

He told her about something called a child contact centre where she might be able to see Mum.

Molly looked astonished.

'Has Mum been there, all the time?' she asked.

'No darling', Dad said 'it's just a place to meet.'

He explained that they'd all go on Saturday and have a look around to make sure it would be OK.

'Just a short visit, like before starting school - but don't get your hopes up, Mum won't be there!'

Molly had walked past the hall lots of times. It had never looked very interesting but today there was a special sign outside.

They rang the bell and were let in.

At a table sat a smiley lady with a badge on saying 'Anne'.

'Hello' she said 'is your name Molly? I'll just tick you off on my list.'

She wrote down what time they'd come and showed them into a waiting room.

There was just one other person in there, drinking tea.

Tommy wanted to get out of the pushchair.
Anne said 'That's fine; leave it here while you have a look around.'

Soon another lady, Su, came in and said 'You must be Molly and Tom; come along in.'

They went into a big room where other children were playing. A wooden railway was left on the floor.

An older boy was sitting talking with his dad.

Molly had a quick check just to make **sure** that Mum wasn't there!

Su said she wanted a chat with Dad, so Molly and Tom could play for a bit.

Tom wanted to sit on Daddy's knee but Molly took him by the hand and although she would have liked to play with the tea things, she knew that Tommy loved trains.

Then Su asked Molly, 'Do you know who you will be coming to see at the centre?'

Wow! Would she really be seeing Mummy here soon? She couldn't wait......

They went for a 'tour' as Su called it, to see another room. It was filled with playthings. 'Can I play here now', Molly asked, 'just for five minutes, **please?**'

'Is that alright?' Dad asked Su.

'Sure' she said, 'what do you fancy Molly?'

Tom still wanted to be held but laughed as Molly put on big tiger feet and wobbled about, holding them by the ropes.

On the way out Su showed them the loos and where to change Tom's nappy.

There was a snack bar selling drinks, fruit, crisps and bars. Su asked if they had any questions but Dad said they'd seen everything thanks and knew what to expect.

At school on Monday her teacher asked what they had done at the weekend. Molly told them about the child contact centre and how she was going to see her Mum there next week.

She was very surprised when Pablo put up his hand and said 'I sometimes go there too, to see my Grandma and Grandpa, not often though 'cause they live in Spain.' Leo said he **used** to go when he was small to see his Dad but now they could meet at the park instead.

Saturday finally arrived; Molly was so excited. Last night Dad had read them a story he'd been given, all about contact centres. It didn't look quite the same as Molly's centre but there were still smiley people in charge and lots of toys!

Today a man called Mike sat at the table and the waiting room was full. Su wasn't there but a helper, Kate, came in to fetch the children, calling out names.

At last she came to them and said 'You must be Molly and Tom, shall we go and see Mummy?'

Dad said 'Tom won't remember his Mum, so is it alright if I come in too?'

Molly dashed in and there, waiting on the other side of the door, with her arms outstretched and tears falling down her cheeks....... was Mummy.

Molly thought she used to be a bit fatter but Mum was smiling despite the tears.

Tommy clung to Dad as they watched Molly and Mum. They all sat down.

After a bit Tom climbed off Dad's knee and started to play with the garage. Mum soon stopped crying and took Molly to get a drink and nibbles. She asked Molly what Tom would like and they bought him raisins and apple juice.

They were talking about school, when a helper came to tell them that it was time to go. They were only booked in for an hour this week.

Mum told Molly how much she had missed her and Molly said 'I've missed you too Mum.'

When she cried, Dad said, 'Maybe we could make it a bit longer next time Moll.'

Mum hugged and squeezed Molly and said 'I'll count the days until I see you again' and Molly said 'I will too.'

Each Saturday Molly and Tom visited Mum at the centre. Soon Tom was happy to go in without Dad. The helper who took them in said 'We all wear badges, so if you are worried about anything, ask one of us and we can speak to Daddy.'

There was no need. Tom and Mummy were getting to know each other now and they all played happily together.

One day in the waiting room Molly sat next to two children with their Dad. 'Are you going to see your Mum?' she asked. 'Yes', they said 'and our little brother and sister too.'

It was ages before she saw them again; they only went to the centre every four weeks.

Once when Dad was waiting, he said that someone hadn't turned up. 'It was awful. That poor little girl was crying and had to go home without seeing her visitor.'

Molly was **so** glad that her Mum came every week.

A lot of children came to see their Dads and the older ones played table football, snooker and table tennis. Sometimes there weren't so many people and they had the art table up, they all loved that.

One day while they were having a story Molly noticed a Dad looking really unhappy because his children hadn't come.

So it's sad for grown ups too thought Molly....

When Tom was poorly one week and couldn't go, Molly remembered the miserable man and then thought about Mum waiting!

She was getting really upset when Dad said 'Hey Moll, don't panic, I've arranged for Grandma to take you. She can go shopping while you're with Mum.'

It felt different without Tom but fun and special too...

They played board games and Mummy did her hair prettily and painted her nails.

Molly made a friend called Sasha; she was the same age and came every week as well. Sometimes the grown ups chatted for a bit while they were getting drinks and the children played together but not for long. Molly really wanted to be with Mum.

Molly noticed that some children who had been coming for a long time were going out with their Dad.

That night when she was having her bedtime drink she asked Daddy when she and Tommy could go out with Mum.

'You will one day sweetheart but for the time being, while Tom is little, why not just enjoy seeing Mum at the contact centre?'

Molly lay and thought about it for a long time and decided that just seeing Mum was the most important thing.

She'd be very happy to carry on going to the centre if that was where her smiling Mum would be.

Did you know that one in three children lose contact with a parent following separation or divorce?

The distress caused by family breakup is often traumatic, heart wrenching and sometimes bitter.
The needs of children during this time are often lost and the pain of losing contact with a mother or father, brother, sister or grandparents is known to have a lasting effect for children in their adult life.

Each year over fifteen thousand children use NACCC child contact centres and services.

NACCC is a national child-centred charity that promotes and supports safe child contact within a national framework of around 350 child contact centres and services.

NATIONAL ASSOCIATION OF
CHILD CONTACT CENTRES

ceprep

Please help us to continue to provide this valuable service by supporting us in this work.

To find out more about our work visit the website at: www.naccc.org.uk or email contact@naccc.org.uk
Tel 0845 4500 280 (local rate) 0115 948 4557 (cheaper from your mobile)

Reg Charity No. 1078636